Oh Golly, Miss Trolley!

BY HAILIE JOHNSON

ILLUSTRATED BY PAWEŁ GIERLIŃSKI

Miss Trolley is excited! Today she picks up Mrs. Breezy's class for her first field trip. She wants the trip to be fun. It's a beautiful but windy spring day as Miss Trolley studies the stops on her map.

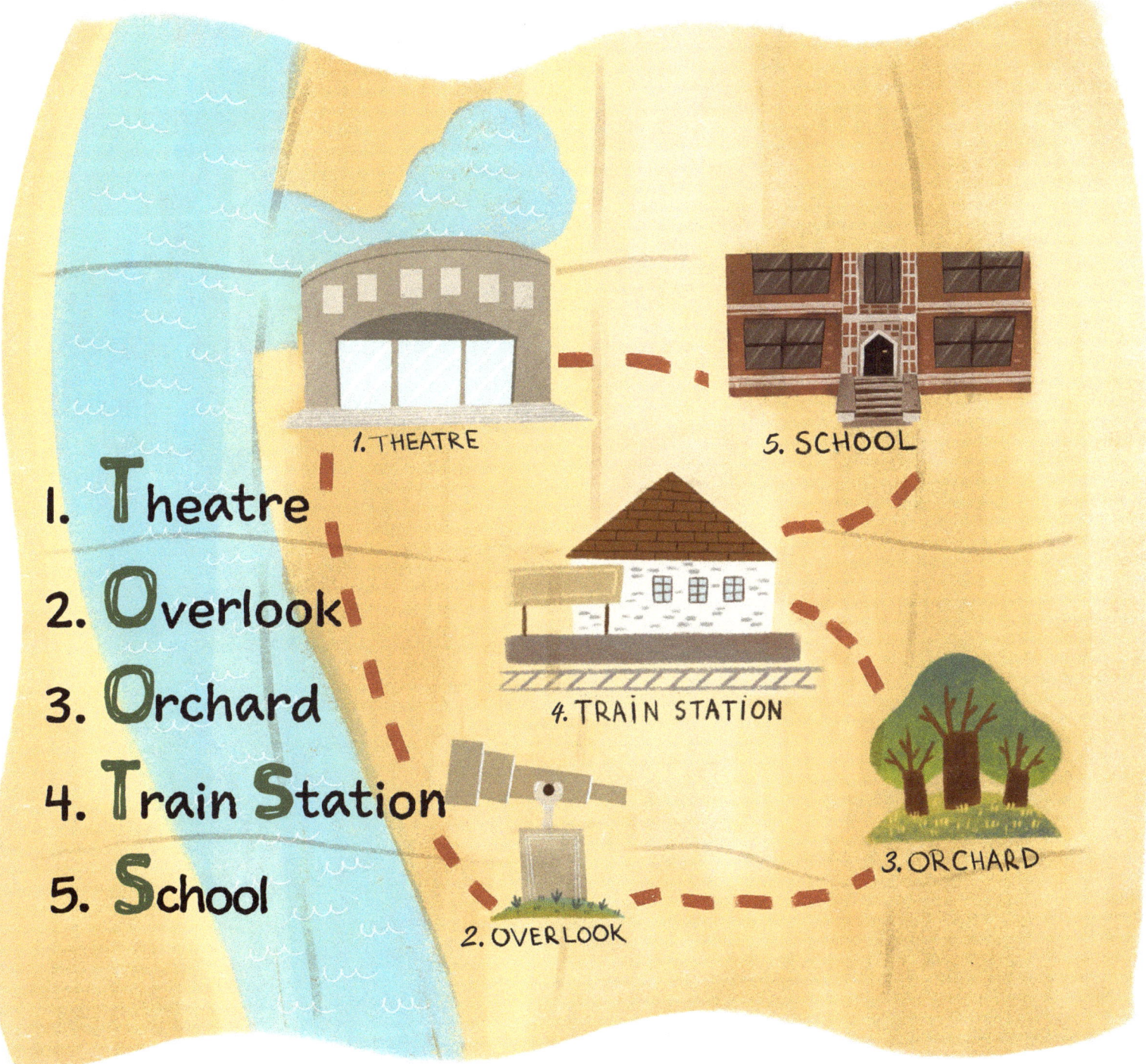

"Wow, what a jam-packed day," Miss Trolley thinks. "How funny—the first letters together spell *TOOTS!*"

Whoosh!

A gust of wind blows the map over the bridge and into the river. "OH NO!" Miss Trolley yells as she slams her brakes.

SCREEECH!

She watches the map float downstream, wondering how she would rescue it... but realizes there's not enough time. Instead, she hustles toward the school to pick up Mrs. Breezy's class.

Miss Trolley's tires SCREECH to a stop outside of the school. Mrs. Breezy's class boards with smiles on their faces.

"How will I ever remember where we're supposed to go?" Miss Trolley worries to herself.

"I think the first stop begins with a T...
Second stop, O...
Third stop, O...
Fourth stop, T...
Last stop, S!"

"That's right,"
Miss Trolley blurts out.
"TOOTS!"

"Time to go, Miss Trolley!"
Mrs. Breezy calls out.
"You betcha!" Miss Trolley says with pep.

Miss Trolley speeds off and arrives at T...

Tea Party Palace

"We're here!" Miss Trolley announces.
"This isn't the *Theatre*," Mrs. Breezy states.
"OH GOLLY, MISS TROLLEY!"
exclaim the kids.

"All aboard! Second stop here we come!"
Miss Trolley shouts with delight.

VARoOM-oOM-oOM

She closes her eyes for a few seconds as she tries to remember the second stop. She revs up her engine at the same time Mrs. Breezy starts talking, so she doesn't hear the next stop.

Then she speeds off, her wheels spinning, and arrives at O…

OBSTACLE COURSE CITY

"We're here!" Miss Trolley calls out.
"Why did you come here?" Mrs. Breezy asks.
"We were supposed to go to the Overlook next."
"OH GOLLY, MISS TROLLEY!" exclaim the kids.

"All aboard for our third stop!" Miss Trolley shouts.
Miss Trolley's bell drowns out Mrs. Breezy's voice as she states the next stop.
She speeds off, swerving side to side, her seats shaking, and arrives at O...

Chirp – Chirp – Chirp

"All aboard! Fourth stop!" Miss Trolley shouts.
The ostrich honks and the children shriek loudly over Mrs. Breezy's instructions. Miss Trolley speeds off in a tizzy, and arrives at T...

Tie-Dye  Treasures

"We're here!" Miss Trolley says.
"Miss Trolley, we are supposed to be at the *Train Station*."
Mrs. Breezy places her hand on her hip.
"You're going to get me in trouble with the parents!"
"OH GOLLY, MISS TROLLEY!" exclaim the kids.

"Miss Trolley, please take us back to school!" Mrs. Breezy pleads. "Sure, you betcha!" Miss Trolley replies.

P...shhhhhhh!

But Miss Trolley has a *better idea*... She releases air from her brakes and parks at S...

"We're here!" Miss Trolley reports.
"Yaay!" The children scream with delight.
"OH GOLLY, MISS TROLLEY!" exclaims Mrs. Breezy.

The trip might not have gone as planned, but it sure was a Totally Outrageous Occasion for Tremendous Silliness! TOOTS!

Published by Orange Hat Publishing 2023
ISBN HC: 9781645384861

Copyrighted © 2023 by Hailie Johnson
All Rights Reserved
Oh Golly, Miss Trolley!
Written by Hailie Johnson
Illustrated by Paweł Gierliński

This publication and all contents within may not be reproduced or transmitted in any part or in its entirety without the written permission of the author.

www.orangehatpublishing.com

For baby Johnson
and all the trolley-loving children.

CPSIA information can be obtained
at www.ICGtesting.com
Printed in the USA
JSHW042331160623
43272JS00007B/87

Made in the USA
Columbia, SC
26 October 2022